To Owen Bahme

Aaron Humphree

RoSco

ALIEN WILDLIFE PHOTOGRAPHER

Drawn and Written by

Aaron L Humphres

For the explorer
in all of us.

FIRST
EDITION

BRYAN SEATON: PUBLISHER/ CEO
SHAWN GABBORIN: EDITOR IN CHIEF
JASON MARTIN: PUBLISHER-DANGER ZONE
NICOLE D'ANDRIA: MARKETING DIRECTOR/EDITOR
DANIELLE DAVISON: EXECUTIVE ADMINISTRATOR
CHAD CICCONI: DROOZY GOO COLLECTOR
SHAWN PRYOR: PRESIDENT OF CREATOR RELATIONS

The "Infinite Safari" arrived at planet Grangawa on the 10th day of our journey.

Our mission was to explore Grangawa and photograph its alien wildlife.

It was a smooth ride all the way down to the surface.

But let me back up and introduce myself.

The name is Rosco and I'm the purple fella.

My shiny robot pal is Vincent.

Together we travel the universe photographing alien wildlife.

You may have seen our photos in Intergalactic Wildlife Magazine.

The robot fellow

The purple chap

We land here to start our journey.

This map shows the route of our expedition.

Budwood Forest

Smud Ponds

Red Rock Grasslands

Sky Reach Peaks

The Infinite Safari travels here on auto-pilot and waits for us.

Googunk Swamp

Egofuls

Our first stop on planet Grangawa was Budwood Forest.

High amongst the treetops lives the colorful Egoful.

It is a very proud bird with a big red beak and pale purple eyes on stalks.

Using a small jet pack, I soared up the Budwood trees.

Soon I spotted an Egoful in its nest.

The Egoful loved having its picture taken.

In fact I could not snap a shot without the Egoful in some sort of pose.

How strange...

Flippery feet.

Beak can ₌ snap ₌ Twigs,

Eyes move on stalks in All directions

Timid Neds

On our second day in Budwood forest, we went in search of Timid Neds.

They are extremely shy creatures with long horns and white fur.

Vincent and I had to improvise in order to get close enough to capture the Timid Ned on film.

Gathering some tree branches and a hollow log, we disguised ourselves.

We found a Timid Ned happily munching on a Pe-Pu branch and quietly approached.

Every time the Timid Ned looked away, we moved closer.

Various ways the horns grow.

Unfortunately, Timid Neds are afraid of trees with cameras.

Next time we should disguise the camera as well.

Hands have webbed fingers

But the feet do not have webbed toes

(I do not know why)

Swinkies

High amongst the trees of Budwood Forest live the Swinkies.

Swinkies are mischievous creatures with three eyes and five tentacles.

They live in small groups known as Smeddles.

I climbed up and snuggled into some branches to wait for the perfect photo opportunity.

I must have dozed off and slipped from my perch, because I awoke in a tangle of vines.

I soon realized that I was surrounded by a smeddle of Swinkies looking at me curiously.

The Swinkies eventually warmed up to me and had a lively time with all my stuff.

All photos courtesy of Swinkies having fun with my camera.

Big flat tongue

Swinkey sleeping

Three suction cups on each tentacle.

Romper Stompers

Outside the Budwood forest lie the Smud Ponds.

In these large ponds of mud live
the Romper Stompers.

These rather large, two-legged creatures have
big eyes and wide mouths.

They spend all day licking up
mud in the ponds.

Most of the time Romper Stompers are peaceful
creatures with gentle dispositions.

Unfortunately, their oversized eyes do not
like bright camera flashes.

At the snap of my camera, they bared their
teeth and chased me away.

Good thing I'm
fast on my feet!

Horns sometimes
twist as they
grow out.

Catuppies

The next day Vincent and I hiked out to the Red Rock Grasslands.

Many creatures out here live underground to stay cool in the warm weather.

One such animal is the six-legged Catuppy.

These curious critters use their strong legs to burrow through the ground and even some rocks.

Catuppies love the fruity lavlets that grow around here.

We gathered up a bagful of Lavlets and headed out to find some Catuppies.

We dangled a Lavlet from a long stick and the Catuppies began to appear from everywhere.

Good thing we had enough Lavlets to go around!

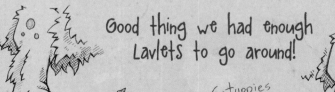

Catuppies walk on their hands

Budoppers

The Red Rock Grasslands have fields of flowers that stretch out in every direction.

Within these flowers live the Budoppers.

I trekked out with Vincent to snap some photos of these critters.

Budoppers camouflage themselves with antennae resembling flowers..

These antenna also serve as their mouths.

The Budoppers will use these flower mouths to suck on anything that looks edible.

Toes, fingers, robot antenna, cameras... whatever draws their fancy.

It took Vincent and I quite a while to remove all the Budoppers after the photo shoot.

3 Toes Per foot.

Green hair tuft looks like grass.

Ooglees

Dusk on Grangawa is the perfect time to find Ooglees in the Red Rock Grasslands.

These animals are rather small with long ears and tufts of fur at the end of their tails.

Ooglees live in underground tunnels that stretch outwards in all directions.

I suited up in my custom Ooglee disguise and confidently strolled into their midst.

My plan was to gain their acceptance, so I could snap photographs without arousing suspicion.

I know I am rather tall for an Ooglee, but my costume was foolproof.

There was no way they could have seen through my disguise.

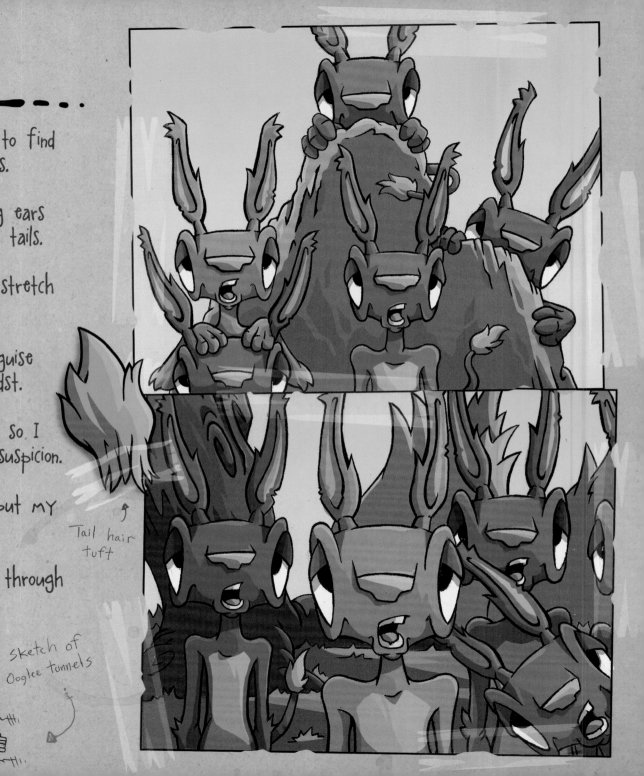

Tail hair tuft

sketch of Ooglee tunnels

Fanlies

The Sky Reach Peaks are home to small flying critters known as Fanlies..

Fanlies flutter around the sky on small wings that twirl like propellers.

The high peaks serve as their home and nesting ground.

I used my trusty inflatable blimp to rise high enough to snap some shots.

A few Fanlies decided to perch on my blimp as I neared their homes.

Soon there were more than a few Fanlies riding along on my blimp.

I quickly realized I'd become a floating lounge for these Fanlies.

Maybe I need to re-evaluate my approach.

Fanlies rub their wings together to make a chirping sound and attract mates

Three long toes

Wing feathers

How the wings start to spin.

Cragocks

The Sky Reach Peaks are home to the towering Cragocks, Planet Grangawa's legendary living mountains.

Cragocks are enormous creatures that spend most of their time hibernating.

In fact, Cragocks spend so much time sleeping that they eventually become covered in dirt and rocks.

Cragocks soon begin to resemble the mountain peaks they dwell in.

This can make spotting them pretty difficult.

Standing Cragock

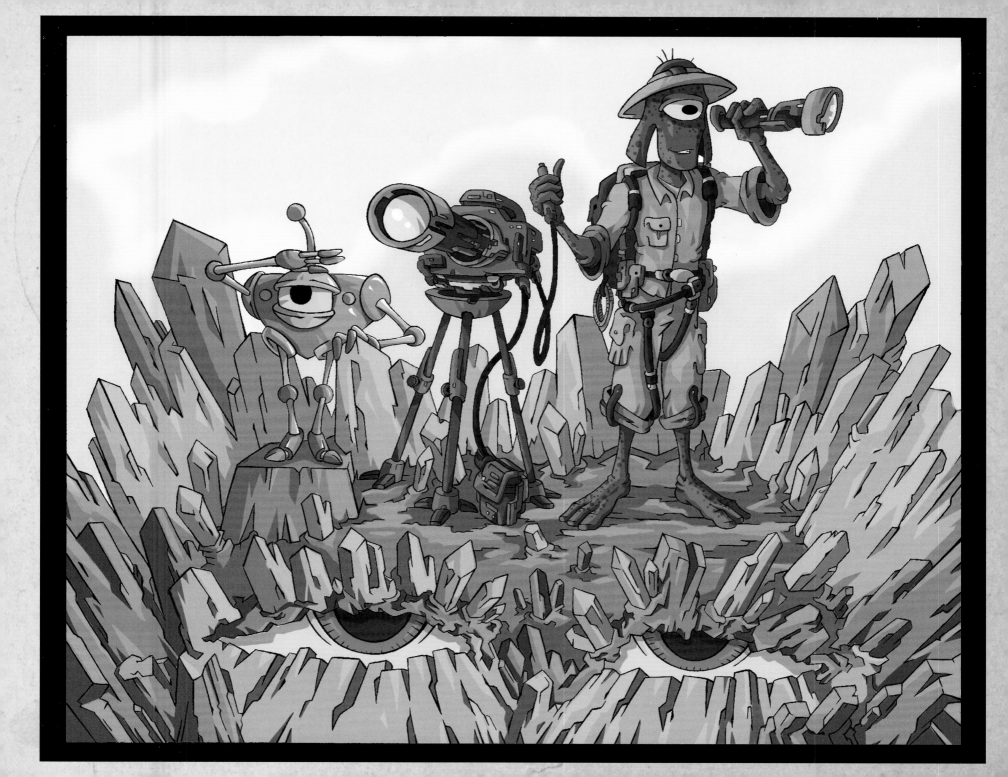

Slickums

Vincent and I spotted a pair of Slickums resting under a cliff as we made our way out of the Sky Reach Peaks.

Slickums are rather large birds with vibrant plumage and very long tongues.

The tongues of Slickums can stretch twice as long as their necks.

They use these tongues to snatch insects out of the air and explore their environment.

Slickums lick everything around them...

...Even purple aliens dangling upside down with a camera.

Colored feathers used to attract mates.

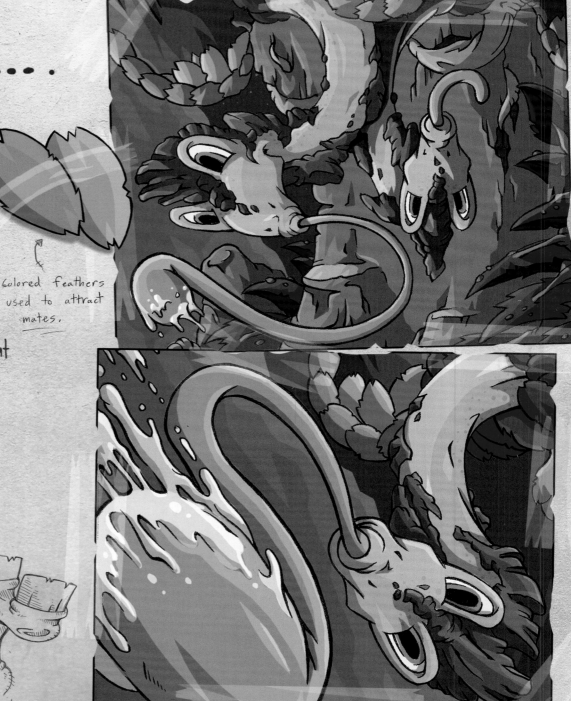

Front of foot.

Slickums hang upside down from one strong foot.

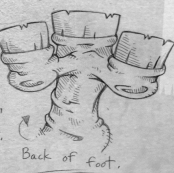

Back of foot.

Reekumps

The final days of our expedition took us to the Googunk Swamp.

Here live large, bloated animals known as Reekumps.

Reekumps float around the swamp all day spewing out stinky gas.

This yucky gas is spewed out of funnels jutting from their backs.

The gas is revolting to anything with a nose, but very tasty to the local plants.

In exchange, the Reekumps eat the plants and algae.

My plan was to approach the Reekump from underwater.

I did not plan on my snorkel becoming a great gas pipe.

Gas rising in blow horn.

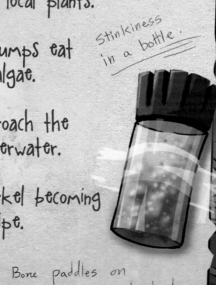

Stinkiness in a bottle.

Bone paddles on bottom of tentacles.

Droozies

The Googunk Swamp is also home to Droozies.

Droozies are small, green lizards with long snouts that live in groups known as Dripples.

These little lizards are very skittish and work together to fend off predators.

They defend themselves by spitting a gooey green slime at anything that startles them.

The slime disgusts the predators, ruining their appetite.

I planned to sneak up on a Dripple before being noticed.

Apparently the Droozies saw me before I saw them.

Now I understand why Vincent brought an umbrella.

One toe longer than other one

Sample of green goo.

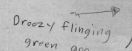
Droozy flinging green goo.

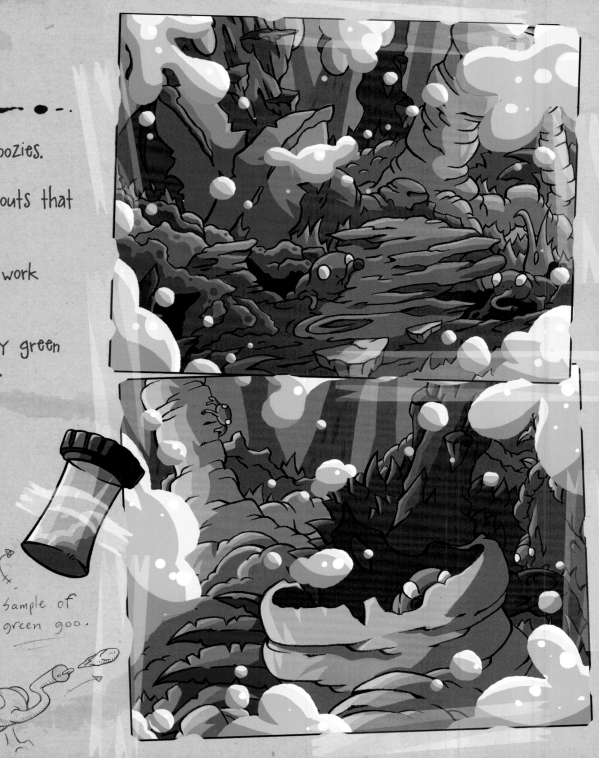

The Snaptron 200

The Snaptron is the cutting edge of camera technology.

Built tough for any field conditions and comes with lots of extra parts.

The lense can be extended super long and bend around all sort of obstacles.

This camera is my most trusted tool on safari.

Multiple size lenses

Extra parts to construct new camera modes for different field needs.

Camera is digital with lots of room to store photos!

Adjustable grip to steady the camera

Infinite Safari

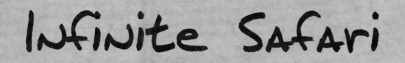

My spaceship the Infinite Safari is specifically designed to fly and land in rough terrain.

The hull is outfitted with a roll cage to protect it.

Topnotch flood lights sit atop the cockpit to light up the densest weather.

All my cameras, gadgets, and survival gear are stowed neatly in the back.

There is even a state of the art entertainment center for those long trips through the cosmos.

The Infinite Safari is my home in the galactic wild.

A sketch of the cockpit controls

Wings bend to help guide the Infinite Safari in atmospheric flight.

ery intense flood lights!

Landing Gears

The underside of my ship.

Reinforced for those rough landings.